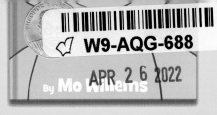

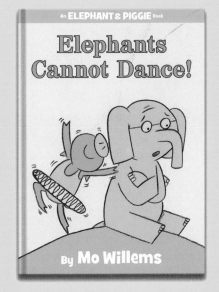

To Sandy Boynton
The master

Text and illustrations copyright © 2020 by Mo Willems.
ELEPHANT & PIGGIE is a trademark of The Mo Willems Studio, Inc.
Elephant & Piggie portrait (page 313) © 2020 by Bryan Collier.

First Edition, September 2020
10 9 8 7 6 5 4
FAC-039745-21363
This book is set in Century 725/Monotype; Grilled Cheese/Fontbros; Typography of Coop, Fink, Neutraface/House Industries
Printed in South Korea
Reinforced binding

Library of Congress Cataloging-in-Publication Control Number: 2020932659
ISBN 978-1-368-05715-8

Visit www.hyperionbooksforchildren.com and www.pigeonpresents.com

An ELEPHANT & PIGGIE
BIGGIE!
Volume 3

An ELEPHANT & PIGGIE Book

There Is a Bird on Your Head!

By Mo Willems

An ELEPHANT & PIGGIE Book

Are You Ready to Play Outside?

By Mo Willems

An ELEPHANT & PIGGIE Book

Elephants Cannot Dance!

By Mo Willems

An ELEPHANT & PIGGIE Book

Should I Share My Ice Cream?

By Mo Willems

An ELEPHANT & PIGGIE Book

I Will Take a Nap!

By Mo Willems

By Mo Willems

Hyperion Books for Children / *New York*

Originally published in September 2007.

There Is a Bird on Your Head!

An **ELEPHANT & PIGGIE** Book
By **Mo Willems**

Hyperion Books for Children / *New York*

10

There is a bird
on my head?

aggghhh!!!

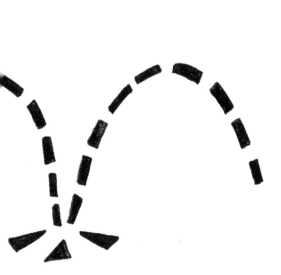

Is there a
bird on my
head now?

No.

They are
in love!

They are love birds!

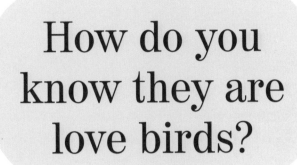

How do you know they are love birds?

They are
making
a nest!

Two birds are making a nest on my head?

I am afraid to ask . . .

You have three eggs
on your head.

42

Now, I have three
baby chicks on
my head!

And two birds
and a nest!

I do not want three baby chicks, two birds, and a nest on my head!

Why not ask them to go somewhere else?

52

Ask them?

Ask them!

53

Okay.
I will try asking.

57

You are welcome. . . .

Are *you* ready
to read this book?

An **ELEPHANT & PIGGIE** Book

Are You Ready to Play Outside?

By **Mo Willems**

Originally published in October 2008.

Are You Ready to Play Outside?

By **Mo Willems**

An **ELEPHANT & PIGGIE** Book

Hyperion Books for Children / *New York*

Gerald!

PLINK!

78

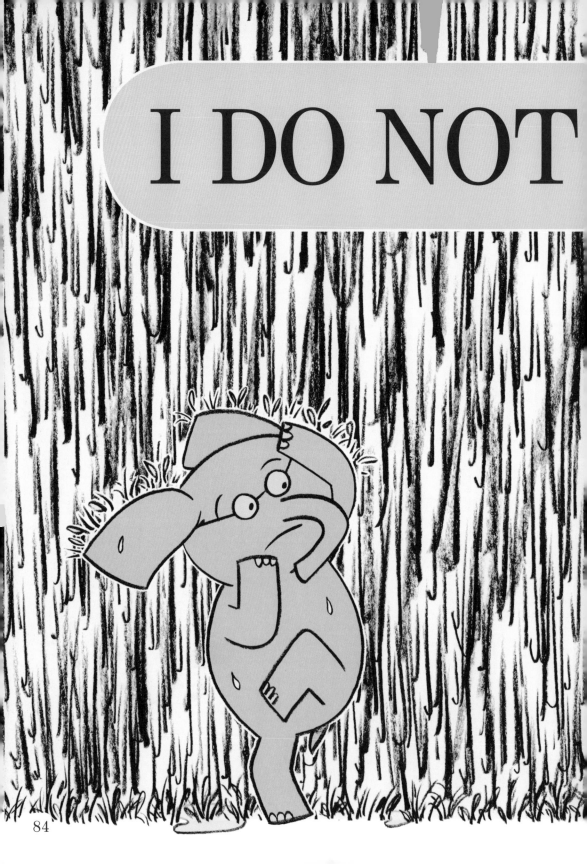

I DO NOT

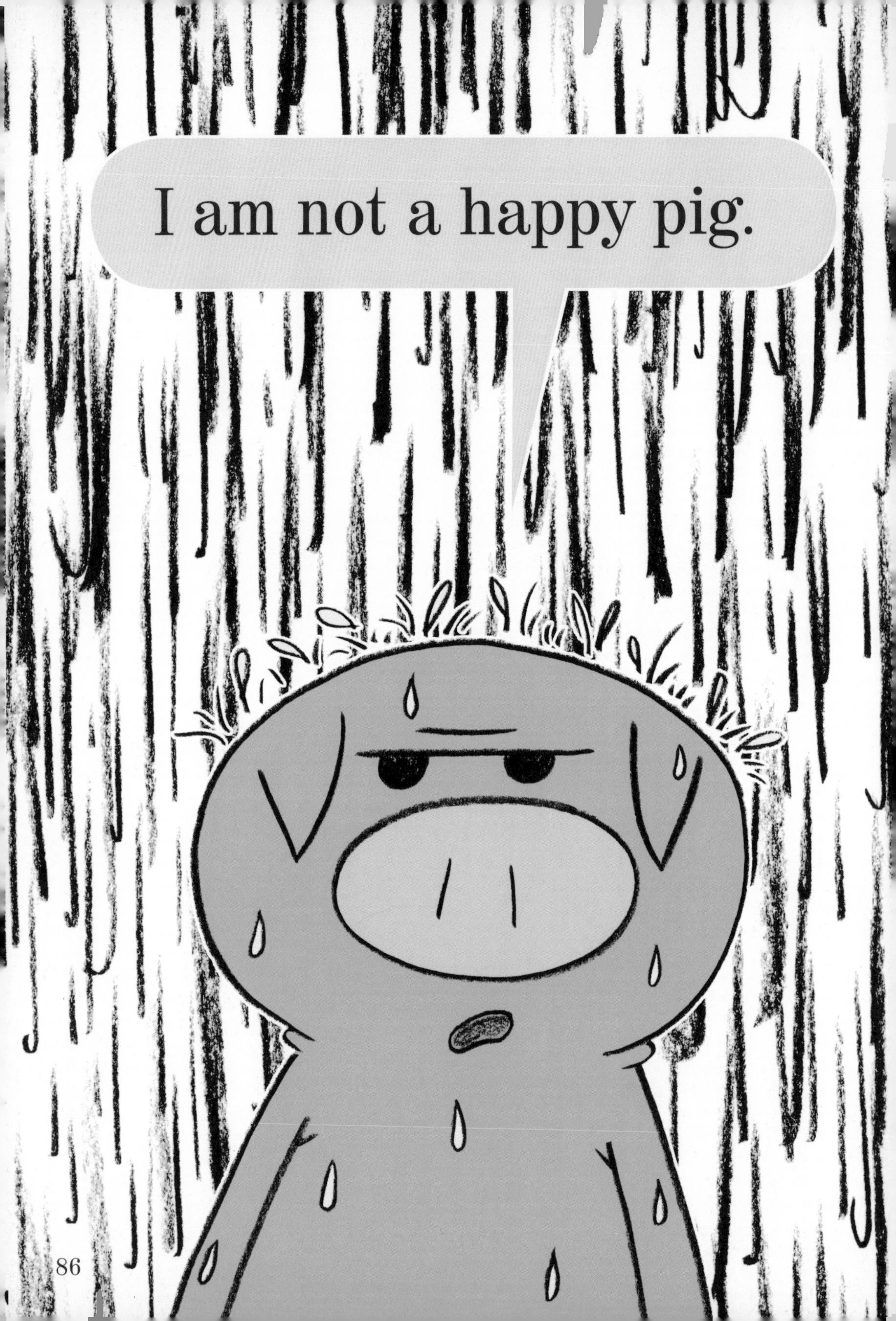
I am not a happy pig.

89

.90

HOW CAN ANYONE PLAY OUTSIDE WITH ALL THIS RAIN!?!

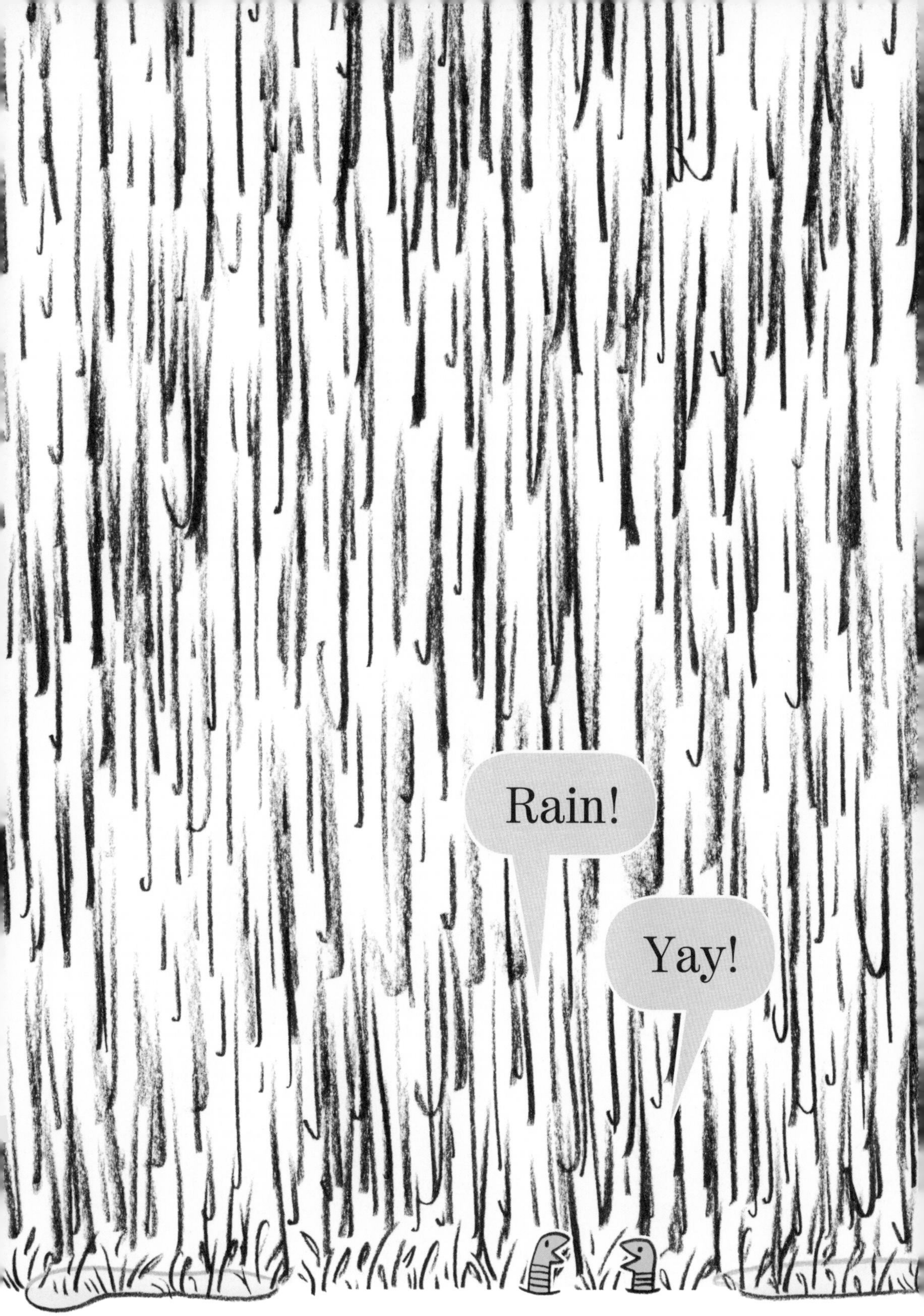
Rain!
Yay!

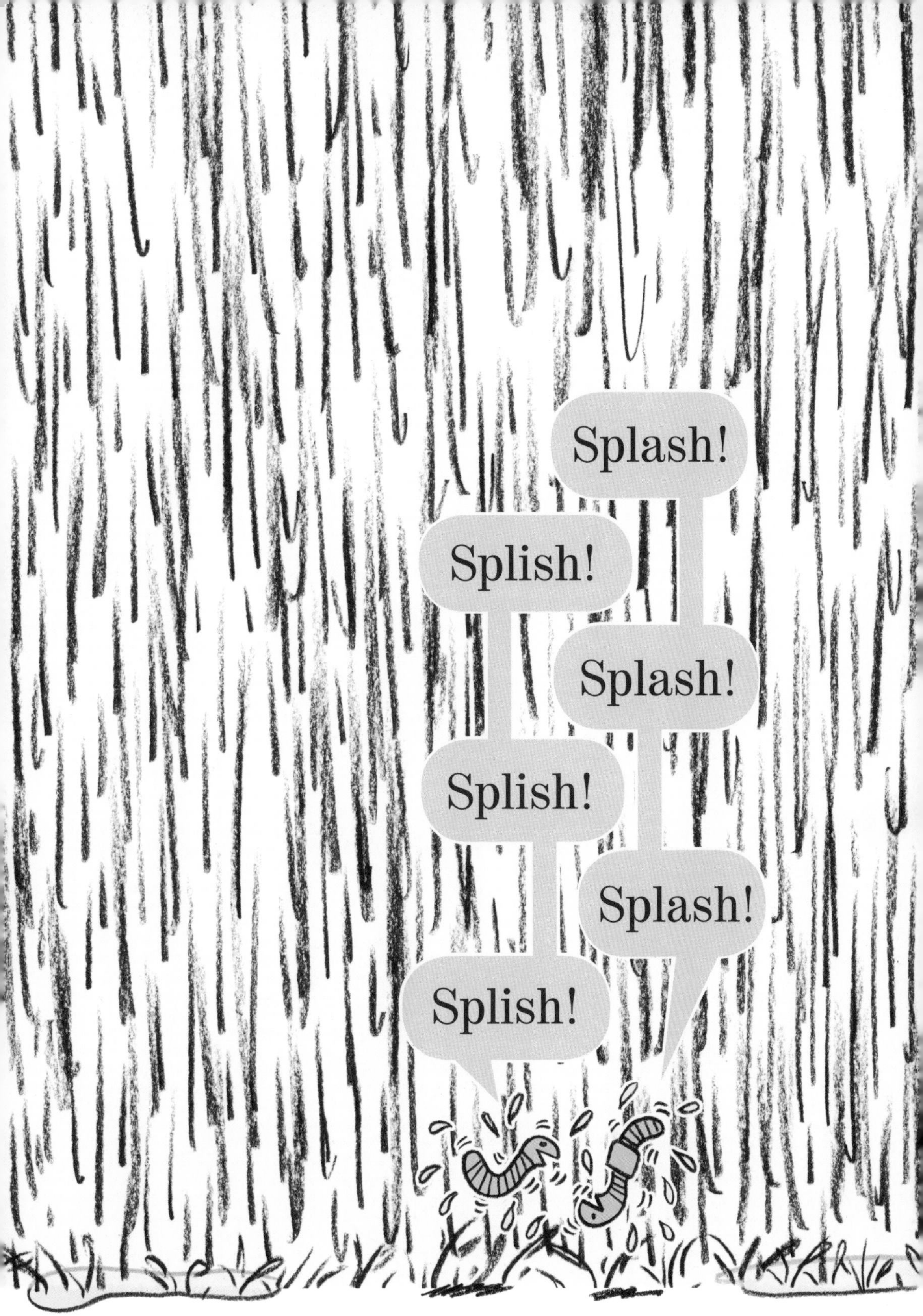
Splash!
Splish!
Splash!
Splish!
Splash!
Splish!

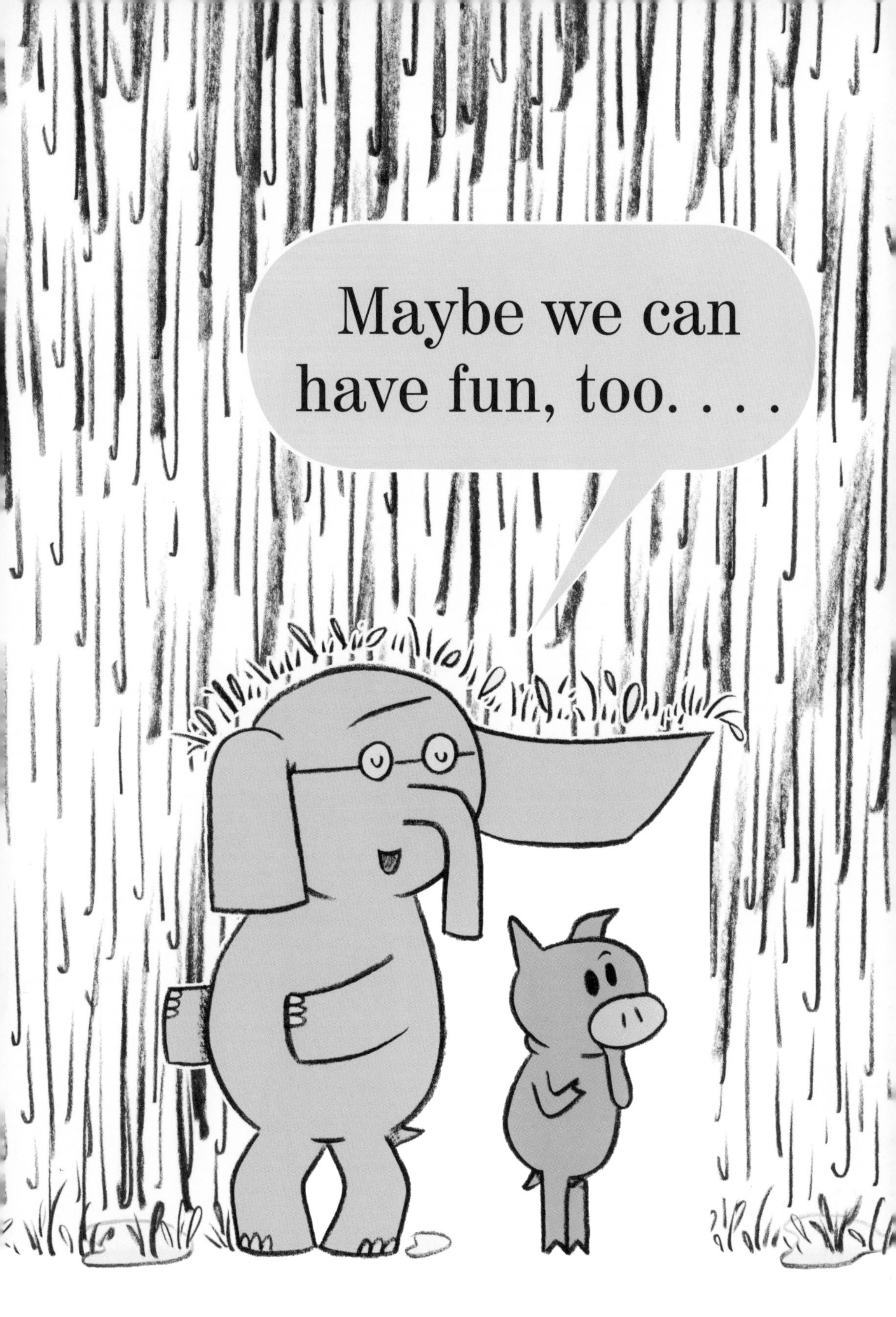
Maybe we can have fun, too. . . .

111

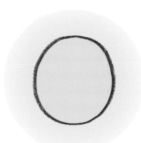

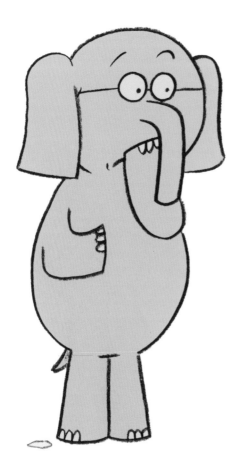

I am not
a happy
pig.

Do not worry, Piggie.
I have a plan.

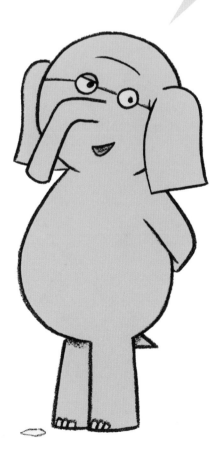

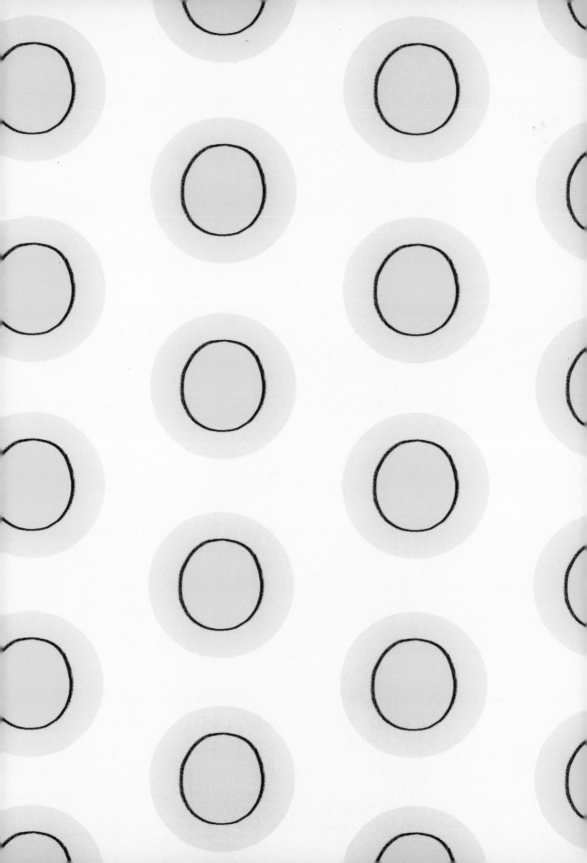

An **ELEPHANT & PIGGIE** Book

Elephants Cannot Dance!

By **Mo Willems**

Originally published in June 2009.

Elephants Cannot Dance!

An **ELEPHANT & PIGGIE** Book

By **Mo Willems**

Hyperion Books for Children / *New York*

Gerald!

131

Let's dance!

I can teach you!

I *will* try to dance!

ZIP!

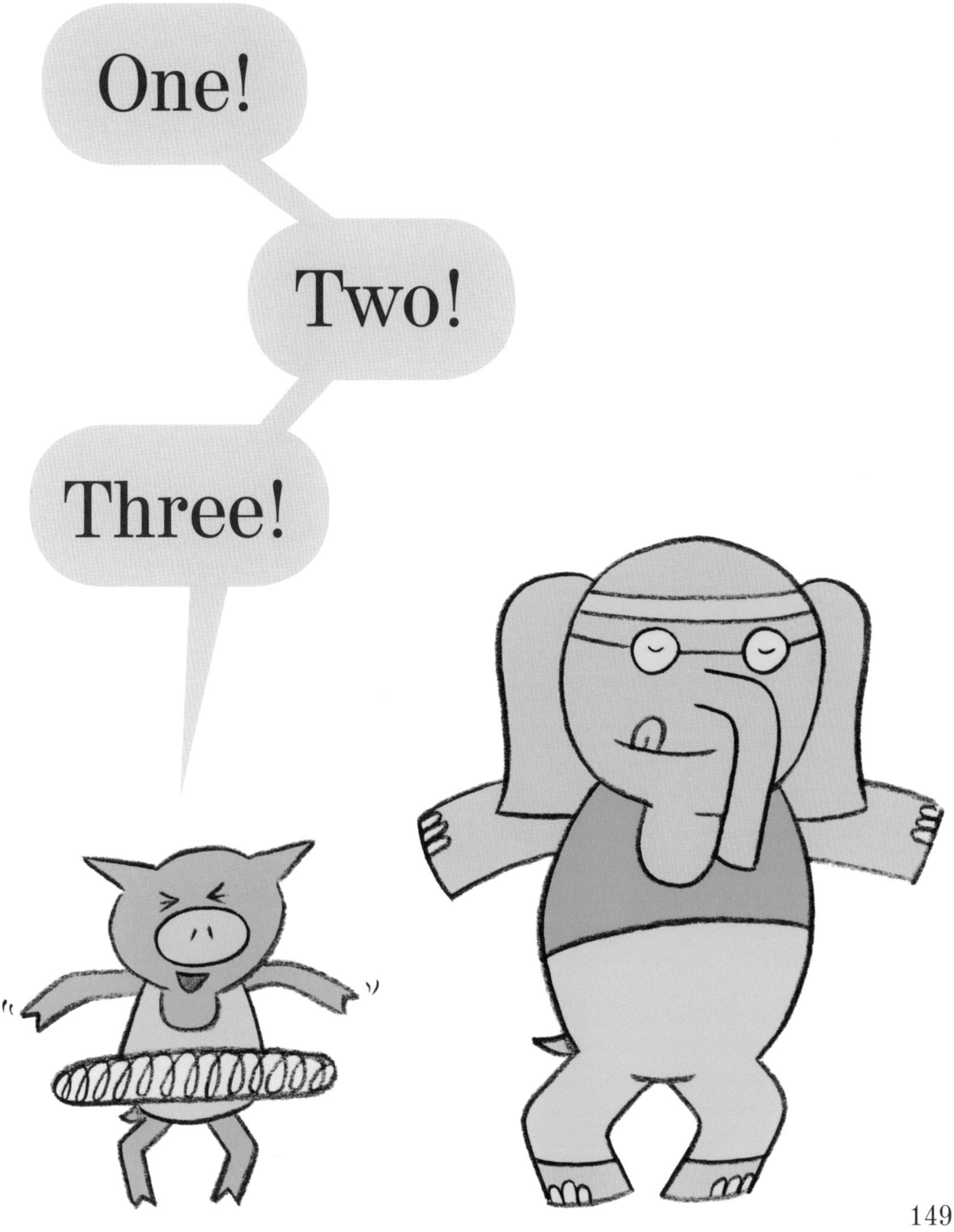
One!
Two!
Three!

We will
try again.

We will
try again.

163

ENOUGH!

171

173

But I am
an elephant.

PLop!

176

Oh, Gerald . . .

Hello-o-o-o-o-o-o!

We are ready to learn some moves!

Silly! We do not want *you* to teach us!

We want to learn "The Elephant"!

181

More feeling!

Keep trying!

This one will melt your heart.

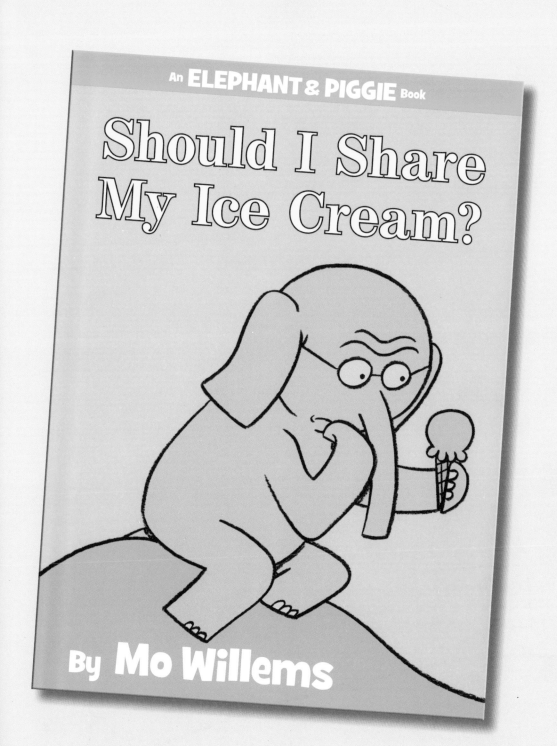

Originally published in June 2011.

Should I Share My Ice Cream?

By **Mo Willems**

An **ELEPHANT & PIGGIE** Book

Hyperion Books for Children / *New York*

Ice cream! Get your cold ice cream for a hot day!

Should
I share my
awesome,
yummy,
sweet,
super,
great,
tasty,
nice,
cool
ice
cream?

217

218

Then she
will say:

226

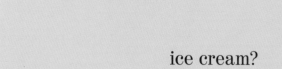

241

243

245

Originally published in June 2015.

An ELEPHANT & PIGGIE Book

Hyperion Books for Children
New York

I Will Take a Nap!

By **Mo Willems**

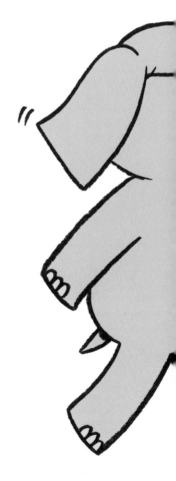

I like to nap.

259

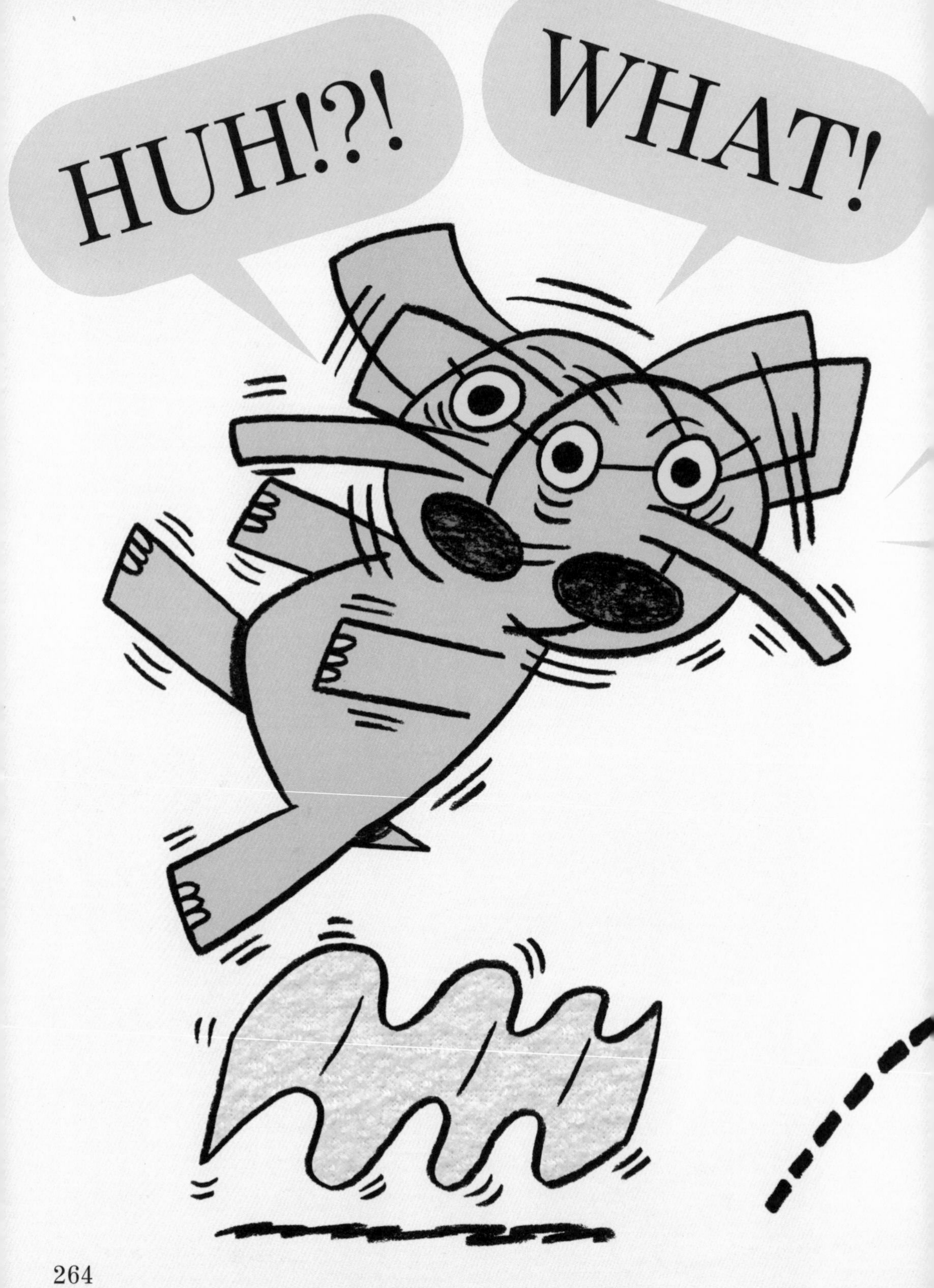
HUH!?!
WHAT!

265

268

269

280

281

294

299

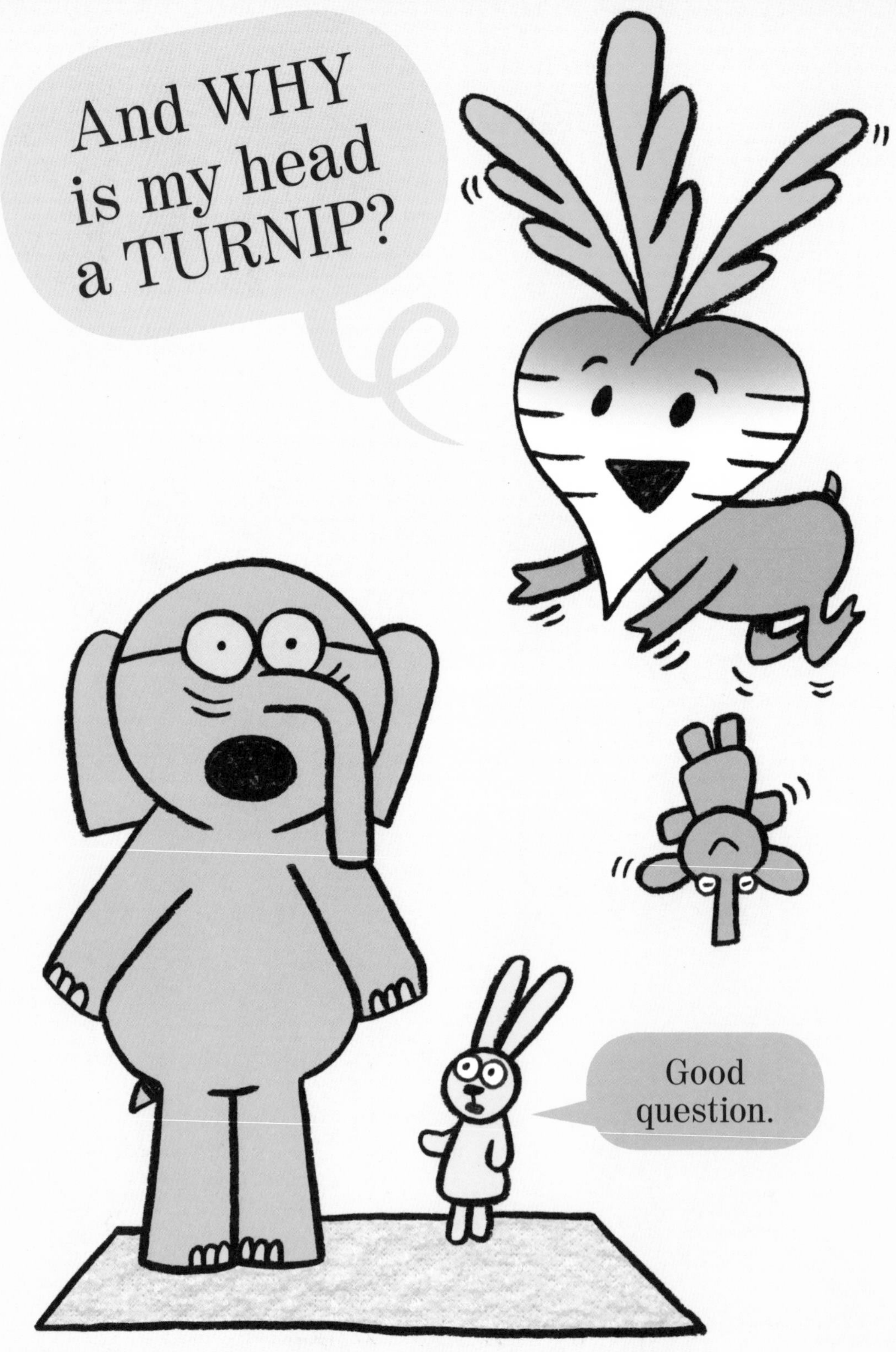
And WHY is my head a TURNIP?
Good question.

304

I'm floating!

Also, I have a TURNIP HEAD!

Dear Reader,

Wow!

You read five Elephant & Piggie adventures in one book! Congratulations!

Reading about how elephants and pigs solve problems is a great way to think about what you would do. (Even though you are probably not an elephant or a pig!) When I was a kid, I liked to read about Snoopy. (Even though I was not a beagle!)

Here's a problem I bet you can solve: How do YOU draw Elephant & Piggie? My friend Bryan Collier drew Elephant & Piggie in his own style. I love it!

Your pal,

Bryan Collier is a six-time Coretta Scott King
Award winner and four-time Honor recipient. He
also has been awarded four Caldecott Honors. Bryan
wrote and illustrated *It's Shoe Time!* an ELEPHANT &
PIGGIE LIKE READING! book. His other books include
Uptown, Trombone Shorty, and *Martin's Big Words:
The Life of Dr. Martin Luther King, Jr.*

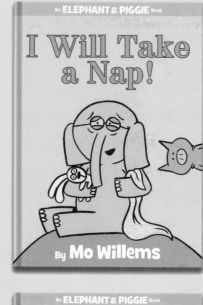